Confessions

Confessions

Vanessa Mills

To order additional copies of this book, contact:
Xlibris Corporation
0-800-644-6988
www.xlibrispublishing.co.uk
Orders@xlibrispublishing.co.uk
301423

Contents

Opening Note

Dear reader,

You are about to witness the confessions of a self proclaimed sinner; baring their soul to the general public. Questions and requests can be made to confessions_no-angel@live.com

Thank you for your time. Here's hoping it's time well spent.

A Haiku

Laying here in bed
Knowing that I'd love your touch
Doesn't help me sleep

A sonnet for the Doubt

I cherish every moment spent with you
For when you're gone I'm feeling blue
My heart, it pounds when you are here,
My body trembles when you are near
A feeling like this, a love so rare
No other feeling can compare
Neither of us is perfect, it's plain to see
But that's the way it's meant to be
We have our fights
And happy nights
But when you're angry
You still know you're the only one for me
So I never will retaliate
As no one else could compensate.

Angels

No, I'm no angel
But you can fall back on me
I'll always catch you

Anna

I need your help
I'll never measure up
This world is corrupt
And so are we
So please
I need to measure up

Take my hand
Before I break
We all need saving
So save me
Stop the pain
Save me.

Backstabber

I'm not deaf
And I'm not blind
I can see all the secrets you hide
In your eyes so deep
Think no one can see all the pain you hide inside
It eats you up to be
So two faced you think no one will know
What I see but I see the truth
Reflecting from your eyes to their eyes going
Back and forth, back and forth inside
Their minds
You wasted it away
All that time you could've had it all but
You're so two faced
They won't even answer your call
How does it feel to know,
We can all see your true colours?
Backstabber.

Blank canvas

Nothing's real,
Nothing was,
I don't feel
And that's because
You took my heart
It broke apart,
Nothing's real,
Nothing was.

Never lie,
Never tell;
Never give your heart,
As well,
You'll never get it back,
Never back intact.

You're my life
But you don't even care
Those promises,
It's like they're never there
Take it all,
Take it back,
Take my life,
Don't want it back.

Nothing's real,
Nothing was.

Cars

Sometimes I overheat and break down
Especially when you're not around
You can fix me up but I'll still break
You can turn me off but I'll still shake
You can strip my paint
But I'll still hate
You can sort that chip
But I'm no saint
Tie me down with your restraint
But I'll still move
And love still waits

CH

Little girl
Little girl, why so sad?
Dry your eyes
I don't want to see them cry, cry, cry
Little girl
Little girl, where did you hide your smile?
It was so beautiful,
It was so beautiful last time I saw it shine.

Christmas time.

Christmas and I'm missing you
Don't know what I should do
I'm so in love with you
You're always on my mind
Could never leave you behind
They say love is blind
So how can I see you?
How do you see me too?

Confessions

I want to go somewhere
Faraway
But still I long
Just to stay

My tartan soul will go to hell
Like the angel Lucifer fell
So I'll live my life
While it lasts
And the past can stay
In the past

Couldn't see the love

He told me that
It wasn't him

But I'm not stupid
And I saw her messages.

Yeah, he told me that
I was blind.

Couldn't see the love
Just couldn't see the love, no.

But I saw her name
Around your neck.
Never been the same since then.

They told me
Love is blind.
But I could see it in your eyes;
Just not when you're looking at me.

Cry

Don't. Hurt. Your. Fragile wrists.
Don't. Cry. No more.
Don't. Be afraid to fall in love,
It's a thing we've got to do
A thing for me and you

Take this hand,
Take this fairytale,
Take this heart
Because now it's yours

Don't. Break. Your. Sin free soul.
Don't. Fear. No more.
Don't. Be the one to live alone,
This life was made for two,
Made for me and you.

Take this hand,
Take this fairytale,
Take this heart
Because now it's yours

Don't. Break. My. Heart.

Dear friend

Dear friend,
You are so beautiful
Inside and out
But you don't see what we see,
You can't see what a star you'll be

Dear friend,
You worry us so,
Your bones stick out from under your skin
Starving for perfection
You never see your true reflection

Dear friend,
Your quest was over long ago
You're so loved and misunderstood
No one sees the pain inside
No one see that pain you hide

But we do. We see it.
We all love you.
Just the way you are.

Desires and Adoration get you Nowhere

All we need is truth
A world without the lies
A world where no one cries

We just want to be held
Tell us it'll be okay
And hold us through the day

We need that little something
A little hope to hold on to
A little love to get us through

Keep me close
Keep me near
Keep me close without a fear
Hold me tight
Hold me dear
Hold me now, before I disappear

End to Begin

All is lost
Yet all is won
I thought it had ended
But it's only just begun

Forever in my heart
Will be a place for you
But now I've escaped the binding prison
That people call 'love'
Now I've escaped
I'm free to roam

The news, I admit, was not a shock
But it still scares me
You see, I could've been your rock
But it's not meant to be

I don't mind though
Life goes on
Time will always be wasted
On people like you

Enigma

You watch her walk by
With an air of mystery
You've heard the rumours
Of woe and misery

Her untellling eyes like droplets in the sea
Her flowing hair glimmers in the light
And those elegant shoes
As deep and dark as the night

But as she walks by . . .
That aromatic scent of perfume
And the shy suggestive smile
It makes you crimson
That she really noticed you
That mysterious solitary maiden

Fairytale Ending?

Looking back on times gone past
Wondering why these memories last
Is this rain on my face?
Or am I crying?

This isn't what I wanted
Always being haunted
By thoughts of leaving you
By thoughts of wanting to

I'm restless
And I'm faithless
But even in the darkness
Hope will always shine

Are these raindrops on my face?
Or am I merely crying?

Folie à deux

So who'd have thought?
The two of us bound
By the madness within.
So who'd have thought?
The two of us bound
By the seventh deadly sin.

When you left
You should've taken this too
When you left
I wished you'd seen us through
Folie à Deux

For you

What do I want to get
For you?

Ask me today
And I will say
Perhaps a squished up spider?
Or a lovely angry tiger?
Ask me yesterday
And I would say
How about a sharpened knife?
Or a guide to better your life?

What do I want to get
For you, my lover?

For you,
A dozen dying roses?
Or a kitten that only dozes?
I could even bake you a cake,
Laced, if your words be fake.

Vanessa Mills

Going for forever

Guess how long I'm going for?
I'm going for forever
You and I were never
Going to stay together

So I'm writing this without you
Wonder if you're going too
Wonder if you'll be true
To anybody ever who
Steps into your life

Now I'm going for forever
And I'm never coming back
Have you ever even
Been keeping track?

Good enough

My coat around these bones
The pain that you will never know
I've been thinking of you
That food it can't sustain
My world cannot revolve
Around you
And we all know . . .

I'm not good enough
I'm not good enough
I'm not okay
Cuz I'm not good enough for you

Shed my skin and form A new
Translucent Natural Bones are waiting
I've been thinking of you
Your arms were so warm around me
Need to go back to that home
Where you kept me from falling
And now suddenly . . .

I'm good enough
I'm good enough
I'm okay
Cuz I'm good enough for you

Yes, I'm a mess
Burning building torn apart
And I guess
You'll take those flames away
Cuz now . . .

I'm good enough
I'm good enough
I'm okay
Cuz I'm good enough for you

———∿∿⟋⟍⟋⟍∿∿———

Her

Tumour. Spreads. Want it to go.
It's driving you away
Please don't go
Not this way

You won't be the first
You won't be the last
Could we put this day
In the long lost past?

She's the tumour in our lives
Eating us up inside
She's the wedge driving us apart
Can you make her go?

There's not long left
And this is theft
Stealing our precious memories
Twisting them beyond recognition
Need a magic mans remedies
To send away our cancer.

———∿∿⟋⟍⟋⟍∿∿———

Hoping, wishing

It's been over ten years now
But it's only just sunk in
You've gone but . . .
It was never your time
I feel inside . . . it was not your time
It hurts so much now
I'm crying over long lost memories
And long-loved photographs
If only there was a way,
Any way
To bring you back
I would do it

Ice

"Your veins are filled with ice
But your manners are oh—so—nice
It only takes one look
For you to hypnotise."

**"You sit upon your throne
And want to be alone
Since the day he left
All you've done is wept"**

"Head held high
Long dark hair
Pale white skin
They ask you if you'd dare
To go against
Everything you've known
To defend the honour
Of your mighty ice cold throne."

Insomnia

The sleeping pills aren't working
And I'm still laying here
Thinking of your suggestions
And ways to get away
From this

That old song that I wrote
The words all fade away inside my mind
The text message you sent
Plays round and round inside my head

The ashtray that I hold
Your cold black leather coat
Hold memories of the good times
Hold memories of the good times
With you

I'm still here in this bed
Remembering what you said
Every word, every word
I hang on to

Because meeting you has made me feel alive
Because loving me was all I had to ask
And loving you was all I ever had

So when the pills don't work
And the morning's rushing in
I'm still thinking of you
Thinking of you
I'll think of you with every breath I take
Until there's no more tears
Left to dry

Vengeance is sweet
I still feel the pain
Knife in my back
Trust in my stomach
Break in my heart.

King of the Castle

Wow. The first day I met you
That's just what I said
We walked beside the sea
And talked, just you and me

'Cause you're the king of the castle

Love. It's what I saw
When I looked deep in your eyes
The deepest, darkest brown
The greatest sight in town

'Cause you're the king of the castle

Nothing. It's what I said
When I found out what you did
Smashed my heart to pieces
Still haven't ironed out the creases

And you're the king of the castle.

Little Columbia

I fell in love with a man on a bike
But he didn't like me the way I'd like
So Frankie took me in
I saw the future in him
But he took away
That man with a grin

He was my hope through the pain
It was love at first sight
Tainted my world with rose
Now I'll never see him again

Such a sad, sad tale
Of such a mad, mad male
He locked himself away
Now I'll never love again

Loss

Such blackened guilt lies heavy on my heart
The love I lost is tearing me apart
Although it seems I cannot find
A reason for my being so blind
They wanted this all along
Now they've got it and it's all my fault

And now within me deep inside
The emptiness that began to hide
Has reappeared and come to play
I cannot take this every day
A spoilt society has ruined it all
Now, I'm left waiting for your call

My Valentine

The day didn't go the way . . .
It didn't go the way you planned.
Lonely again on the day of love.
A dying rose
It withers in your grip
A tear forms
Forms and falls down your pretty face
You hear footsteps
What does it matter now?
A gentle hand on your shoulder
As your tears bring the rose to life
She kisses your lips softly
And you'll know, you're where you belong.

Passion

Pick the right flowers
And always keep them close
Someday you're going to make them proud
Someday you're going to be allowed
In your heart your dreams are strong
Only you can fulfil them
Now I wrote your song

Plans—a haiku

Your words touch my soul
Keeping a smile on my face
Me and you against the world

Player

The smile on your face
Is always in place
It makes me grin
'Cuz I know this is sin

You hurt me once
You hurt me twice
You hurt me again
And I won't be nice.

You've taken the stage
And minimum wage
For the hundredth time
So please the crowd
Who you can't live without.

Prince

He holds you close
Breathing lightly
You think you're in heaven
With visions so slightly

His dark brown eyes like chocolate fountains
His ravishing curls . . . cupid shot his arrow
And his skin tight jeans
Surround his legs so narrow

But as he holds you . . .
His soft firm grip
Gentle lips brush your neck
Your legs start to shake
Luckiest girl in the world
You know he'll look after you.

Radio girl

She plays that radio so loud
But it's not the song she's singing
Because living is easy with your eyes wide shut

She's never going to make it through
And that's the truth
And she said, she said
"I'm no good for you, my poison it kills like a curse"
Yeah, she said, she said:
"I only make things worse."

She plays that radio so loud
But it's not the song she's singing
Because living is easy with your eyes wide shut

The clouds are stalking her
Watching every move she makes
Watching every second spent with you
Her life is an empty well
He throws pebbles in, making wishes,
Just making wishes

She plays that radio so loud
But it's not the song she's singing
Because living is easy with your eyes wide shut

Remember

Today is the day
The day we remember
All those brave souls
Who gave their lives away

Have your minutes' silence
Say your little prayers
Why don't we just stop
All the worldwide violence?

Today has gone away
But we won't forget
We will always remember
This eleventh day

Ridicule and wonder

We should both be happy now
We got what we wanted
But is it what we wanted?
What we truly wanted?
Is there more to this?
Is there more than meets the eye?
Do I want you?
Do you want me?
Or do I want someone else?
Do you want something else?
You're always there
I'm not all there
Something is definitely not right

Say my name

I feel the truth inside
But my mind likes to differ
From the truth so clear
The truth I hear
Whenever you call my name.

I feel the shiver
In my bones
Having you near
Erases my fear
Whenever you whisper my name.

My mind can lie
But my heart does sing
This must be true
How I feel with you
Whenever you say my name.

Scarlet slumber

Morally, your love is tainted
By the colour that you paint it
Oh, when will your brown eyes see?
What you've done to me?

Down inside you're hurting
A troubled childhood emerging
You're like a little lost boy
Searching for a lost toy

Your voice could melt their stony hearts
Your children would be masters of the arts
You never know what's inside
Unless you take it for a ride

Sister, Sister

Hey little sister,
Why so sad?
Hey little sister, don't be mad.
You know i love you,
You know i miss you,
Come take my hand,
Please try and understand.

Your pretty little face
Comes back to me in my dreams.
So much we bothe have to say,
But never find the words, it seems.
I'll never say goodbye,
Only bon voyage.
But baby, please don't cry,
Dry those tears.
Don't ask why,
Just be happy.

—————

Soldier of our time

Mighty warriors
From here to there
Because for us, they do care
Defending men beneath deaths stare
They fought for us.

Injured soldiers
Battle on
Making sure to right the wrongs
Helping others, fixing things
They fought for us.

Miles from home
Saving innocent people
Kneeling before the mighty steeple
We must be sure to thank,
They fight for us.

—————

Starts in the sky

Raindrops on the window
Pain.
There's nothing but the sound of rain,
No light breathing in my ear,
Not a sign that you were here.

Take me back
Into your arms
Take me back
Away from harm.

That way

You're afraid of losing him
They all see it in your eyes
And your love runs so deep for him
He feels it in the . . .

The way, the way
You whisper in his ear
The way, the way
The way you hold him near
The way, the way
You swear that you won't disappear

So take a step back
Take a look at the situation
Everything is perfect just the way it is
No more, no less
Touching, touching fingertips
Does this seem like you?

He's afraid of hurting you
They all see it in his eyes
And he wants to spend every second with you
You feel it in the . . .

The way, the way
You whisper in his ear
The way, the way
The way you hold him near
The way, the way
You swear that you won't disappear
The way, the way

He hurts himself for you
The way, the way
He swears he loves you too
The way, the way
He'll never let you go

So take a step back
Take a look at the situation
Everything is perfect just the way it is
No more, no less
Touching, touching fingertips
Does this seem like you?

You both spend too long
Too long
Being afraid, being ashamed
You spend too long
Too long
Wishing you were never apart

The way, the way
You whisper in his ear
The way, the way
The way you hold him near
The way, the way
You swear that you won't disappear

The note

We've been doing
This for months
Ever since that
Fateful night
Secret 'I love you's'
And promises
But it's all just
Kiss and tell
Written on a note
I <3 you

The way you are

I thought you'd changed
I really did
But nothing's changed
You're still just a kid

So what you look different?
So what your words have changed?
We both know it wasn't love
You betrayed us all
You turned green when
My true love returned

The way you were

Last time I saw you
I was scared
All these months later
I was prepared
Now I know
You're just the way you were
When I first loved you

You look changed
Your face is softer
Your hair longer
Your touch is more gentle
Just the way you were
When I first loved you

You speak with a softer tone
Now I'm not alone
Everything changed
But not what we had
It's just the same
As the way we were
When I first loved you

To you

To the friends who never cared
To the strangers who always stared
To the family who never understood
To the ex who never ever could . . .
To the voices inside my head
To the talking toys inside my bed
To all the things I should've said
To all of you who wish I was dead
I hope you're happy
'Cause I sure am.

Too late

Because i'm sick and tired of
All you rlying
But i cant deny you
Keep my flying
And i know
I know you
Always felt this way
So corrupted
So deluded
In your mind so cold like ice
I see it in your eyes
Its too late,
Just too late.

Untitled

Can't you just stay a while?
Hear me out, hear me shout.
Can you hear me crying?
You once said about tears
In the ocean
Now those tears are mine
Do you remember that scar?
I kept my promises
It's still there, plus more
You stole my soul
All I have is love.
Emptiness.
Memories and scars.
They will never leave me.
Never.

Whatever your crime

You said we're together
From now until forever
Forever lasts for never
All I needed was you
Needed you to need me too
I know you say you do
But is that a lie?
Eye for an eye.
I didn't ever want to say goodbye
You know this makes me cry
So why'd I even try?

Vanessa Mills

Without again

I changed my mind today
Decided I want to stay
I have too much to lose
And offers I can't refuse

I skipped that party today
Decided I want to stay
'Cause I was thinking about last night
And the tunnel I saw through the light

I had a choice today
To tell the truth or lose your smile
If only for a while
But see, I lost my style

I changed my mind, you know
Decided I need to go.

That sound in the wind
Is my heart breaking apart.
You took everything I had
And threw it in the bin
But that's the way it goes
This is my life
I shouldn't have expected any
different
But I did
I looked in our reflection
In your bedroom mirror
Thought I saw love
My mistake.
What did I see?
Because you know that
I'll always come back for you.

Acknowledgements

Wow, two books in just a few months; and what crazy months they've been! First thanks naturally are to anyone that made this possible; everyone at Xlibris for all their help, they've been great! Mums and Dad, without who I'd never have been born ☺ my brothers Jay and Stuart, and of course my little sister! My granddad Kenneth Elkins, Nan and Brian. The Helen's, Kelly, Kira and the kids. My amazing, beautiful friends Saffron Newell-Price, Conor Harkness, Jonathan Wilson, Ashley Mayo, Tom Williams and Tiff for looking out for one of my closest friends ☺also everyone else who has stood by me <3 The awesome, gorgeous Tom Middlecoat <3 Bebedora and Gary for being epic. Just generally epic ☺

Anyone who has served as inspiration for any stories, lyrics, poems or anything else I've written ☺ all the great writers that have been good enough to publish their work for people like me all over the world to read.

All the amazing artists I've listened to who've kept me focused and on the right path (Kind of).

I think the most important thing is that this book is for anyone that can relate to it. I wrote a lot of this a long time ago when I've been down throughout the years.

This book is also for anyone who said I'd never make it, anyone who said I couldn't do it, and anyone who said I'd fail and never make anything of my life ☺

I think that's about it, I'm really sorry if I've forgotten anyone; next time!!

Lightning Source UK Ltd.
Milton Keynes UK
176274UK00001B/15/P